Disney Junior

Vampirina

GOING BATTY

ADAPTED BY **CHELSEA BEYL**   BASED ON THE EPISODE WRITTEN BY **CHRIS NEE**

ILLUSTRATED BY THE **IMAGINISM STUDIO** AND THE **DISNEY STORYBOOK ART TEAM**

ABDOBOOKS.COM

Reinforced library bound edition published in 2020 by Spotlight, a division of ABDO PO Box 398166, Minneapolis, Minnesota 55439. Spotlight produces high-quality reinforced library bound editions for schools and libraries. Published by agreement with Disney Press, an imprint of Disney Book Group.

Printed in the United States of America, North Mankato, Minnesota.
042019   092019

Library of Congress Control Number: 2018966030

 THIS BOOK CONTAINS
RECYCLED MATERIALS

Publisher's Cataloging-in-Publication Data

Names: Beyl, Chelsea, author | Nee, Chris, author. | Imaginism Studio, illustrator | The Disney Storybook Art Team, illustrator.
Title: Going batty / by Chelsea Beyl and Chris Nee; illustrated by Imaginism Studio and The Disney Storybook Art Team.
Description: Minneapolis, Minnesota: Spotlight, 2020. | Series: Vampirina
Summary: Vee is the new ghoul in town and can't wait to make some human friends, but she worries they won't want to be her friend if they learn her secret.
Identifiers: ISBN 9781532143007 (lib. bdg.)
Subjects: LCSH: Vampirina (Television program)--Juvenile fiction. | Vampires--Juvenile fiction. | Friendship--Juvenile fiction. | Children's secrets--Juvenile fiction. | Bats--Juvenile fiction.
Classification: DDC [E]--dc23

DISNEP **PRESS**
Los Angeles • New York

ABDO
Spotlight
A Division of ABDO
abdobooks.com

VAMPIRINA HAUNTLEY IS EXCITED! Her family just moved from Transylvania to Pennsylvania. They're a little bit different from the other families in the neighborhood. That's because Vampirina and her family are **VAMPIRES**!

Vampirina unpacks the last box of cobwebs.

"It sure looks SPOOKY in here," she says.

"IT FEELS LIKE HOME!"

Now that they're all settled in, Vee is excited to make new friends.
Her friends Demi the ghost and Gregoria the gargoyle came with them
from Transylvania, but Vee wants to make some human friends, too.

"Just remember that sometimes humans can be a little jumpy," says Vee's mom, Oxana. "Or screamy," says her dad, Boris. They explain that people are sometimes scared of things they haven't seen before. After all, Vee and her family are the first friendly vampires to live on the block!

Just then, the doorbell shrieks. **EEEK!**
It's their neighbor Edna. She welcomes the Hauntleys to the neighborhood with a plate of yummy cookies. "Welcome to our home, scream home," says Boris.

But when Edna walks inside, she gets a bit of a surprise.
"OH, MY!" she exclaims when she sees Gregoria take a big stretch.
"THAT STATUE! IT MOVED!" Edna cries.

Then she bumps into Penelope, Vampirina's pet plant. Penelope opens her mouth wide.

"AHHH!"

shouts Edna, flinging her plate of cookies into the air. Edna is so spooked she runs right out the door!

"Uh-oh," says Vee. "Humans *are* jumpy. And screamy, too!" Now Vee is worried that making new friends will be harder than she thought. And when Vee gets worried, she gets the battys!

POOF!

Vee turns into a bat!

POOF!

Then a girl!

POOF!

A bat!

POOF!

Then a girl!

"Don't worry," says Oxana. "All vampires get the battys when they're nervous."

Vee looks down. "But I'm scared that I won't make any friends in Pennsylvania."

"Of course you'll make friends," says Oxana.

"But you won't make them in here," adds Boris. "So why not go outside and play?"

Feeling better, Vee gives her parents a big hug. She's ready to give it a try.

Vampirina and Demi go outside to play. "Let's show the human world how lovable you are," says Demi.

Just then, Vee spots the kids next door. **"DEMI, HIDE!"** she whispers.
Demi quickly darts behind a tree so he won't spook them.

The boy points to Vee's house.
"It's **TOTALLY HAUNTED**!" he says.

"No, it's not," the girl insists, rolling
her eyes. Then she spots Vampirina.
"I know! Let's ask her!"

The kids walk to the fence. "Hi, I'm Poppy. And this is my brother, Edgar."
"I'm Vampirina. I just moved in!" says Vee with a smile.
"My brother thinks your house is haunted!" Poppy says.
Vee laughs nervously.
"So why don't you invite us over to prove that it's not?" suggests Poppy.

Vee can't believe her neighbors want to come over to play! "Sure! C'mon over to my totally *not* scary and definitely *not* haunted house!" she says.

But when Vee opens the front door, it makes a big CREEEAAAAK!

"Hear that?" says Edgar. "That is *classic* haunted house!"

Vee takes Poppy and Edgar to her room and shows them her favorite dolls from Transylvania.

"This is Ghastly Gayle," says Vee. "And I love Creepy Caroline. She wears her hair in serpent braids." Poppy thinks Vee's dolls are different—and really fun.

But Edgar doesn't want to play with dolls. He wants to see something **SPOOKY**, so he leaves.

Thinking the humans are gone, Demi pops through the wall. "Hi, Vee!"
But then he spots Poppy.

"GHOST!" Poppy shrieks.

"HUMAN!"
Demi shouts.

"OH, NO!" says Vee,
getting another case of the battys!

POOF!

"AHHHH!
BAT!" shouts Poppy.

"It's just me, Vampirina!" Vee says quickly.
"I didn't mean to scare you."

Poppy is startled—and a little
confused. "You're . . . **A BAT**?"

"Sometimes. Not always," says Vee.
"But it *is* kinda fun to fly." She swoops
and soars around the room.

Poppy smiles. Having a friend who can turn into a bat might be kind of neat!
Just then, Edgar comes back. He heard Poppy scream. "Is it a one-eyed goblin?
Or a mummy in the closet?" asks Edgar excitedly.

Before Edgar sees her as a bat, Vee turns back into a girl. "You can tell him, Poppy," she says quietly.

"Oh, that was nothing," says Poppy. "I screamed because . . . Vee and I both love Justin Teether and the Singing Sirens!"

"Aww, man!" Edgar says, disappointed. "Call me if something spooky happens. I'm out!"

"So you still want to be my friend?" asks Vee.

Poppy shrugs. "I wanted to be your friend before you turned into a bat, so why wouldn't I want to be your friend afterwards, too?"

Vampirina smiles and then gives her new friend a big hug. It looks like making friends in Pennsylvania isn't so scary after all.